The Best Way to Play

by Bill Cosby

Illustrated by Varnette P. Honeywood

SCHOLASTIC INC.
Cartwheel ·B·O·O·K·S·®

New York Toronto London Auckland Sydney

Library of Congress Cataloging-in-Publication Data

Cosby, Bill, 1937-
    The best way to play / Bill Cosby ; illustrated by Varnette P. Honeywood.
        p.   cm.— (A little Bill book)
    "Cartwheel books."
    Summary: Little Bill and his friends, avid fans of the television show "Space Explorers," clamor to get the video game version, but they find that they have more fun using their imaginations while playing outside.
                        ISBN 0-590-95617-5
    [1. Imagination— Fiction. 2. Play— Fiction. 3. Video games— Fiction.] I. Honeywood, Varnette P., ill. II. Title. III. Series. IV. Series: Cosby, Bill, 1937- Little Bill book.
PZ7.C8185Be   1995
[E] — dc20   96-32792
                                                                                            CIP
                                                                                            AC

10 9 8 7 6 5

Printed in the U.S.A.
First Scholastic printing, September 1997

To Ennis,
"Hello, friend,"
— B.C.

To the Cosby Family,
Ennis's perseverance against the odds
is an inspiration to us all,
— V.P.H.

Dear Parent:

Most American children spend three or four hours a day watching television and playing video or computer games. Yet pediatricians and child psychiatrists are urging parents to limit electronic entertainment to a total of two hours a day. This includes even educational TV and interactive videos.

The problem is, when children spend too much of their day sitting in front of a screen, they miss out on the all-important social and intellectual development they can get only through active play with family members and other children. They don't develop their own rich imaginations. And they set themselves up for obesity and other health problems that come with physical inactivity.

In *The Best Way to Play*, Little Bill shows your child a way to use television as a springboard for creative play. After he and his friends watch the cartoon *Space Explorers*, they create their own make-believe spaceship and pretend to be explorers themselves. After a while, they realize it's more fun to play their own game.

The story makes another point, as well. Because younger children don't understand advertising hype, they relentlessly badger their parents to buy the toys and games they see promoted on children's programs. (If they'd only apply that persistence to chores or homework!) Often, of course, the actual merchandise disappoints them. Though Little Bill's parents summon the strength to say no, his friend does get the *Space Explorers* game. And the kids are quickly bored with it.

Most children need their parents' help and encouragement to discover the satisfaction of using their own imaginations. But the rewards of children's active, creative play last a lifetime. *The Best Way to Play* offers your child an example of a great way to have fun — using TV instead of being used by it.

Alvin F. Poussaint, M.D.
Clinical Professor of Psychiatry,
Harvard Medical School and
Judge Baker Children's Center,
Boston, MA

Chapter One

Hello, friend. My name is Little Bill. This is a story about me and my friends.

It was early Saturday morning. All of the grown-ups were busy doing grown-up things. My friend Andrew and I were watching cartoons.

"Hey, kids, this is Space Captain Zeke with some big news . . ."

Andrew and I jumped up and yelled the special saying: "SPACE EXPLORERS RULE!" We saluted and listened closely.

"Are you a Space Explorer?" Space Captain Zeke asked.

"Yes, Captain!" we answered.

"Then stay tuned. *Space Explorers* will be on in one hour."

"That's the best show," I said.

"Sure is!" said Andrew.

"Let's play Space Explorers until it comes on."

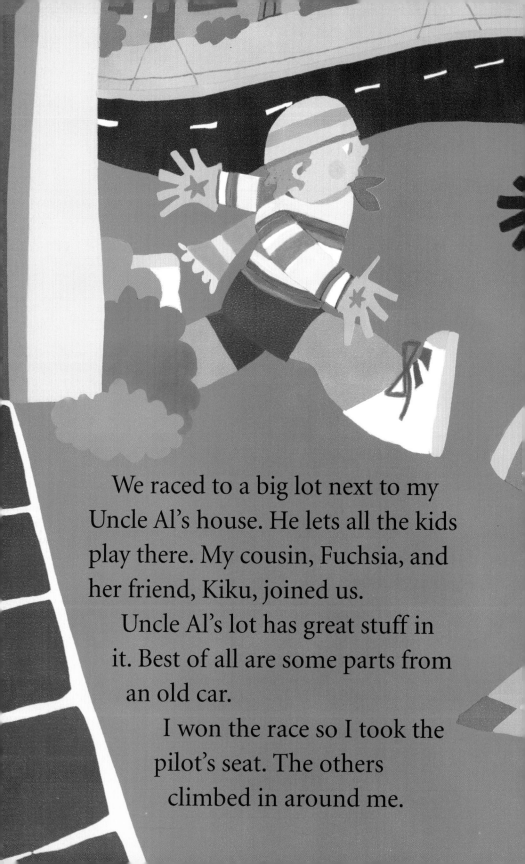

We raced to a big lot next to my
Uncle Al's house. He lets all the kids
play there. My cousin, Fuchsia, and
her friend, Kiku, joined us.

Uncle Al's lot has great stuff in
it. Best of all are some parts from
an old car.

I won the race so I took the
pilot's seat. The others
climbed in around me.

Soon we were in outer space. A white paper bag flew through the air.

"Look out for the meteor," I warned.

We landed on a planet far, far away and climbed out to explore.

Fuchsia caught an alien pet. Suddenly, the owner of the alien pet found us. I had to save my friends.

"Back to the spaceship!" I shouted. "We have to get away before the monster alien gets us!"

We ran back to our spaceship just in time. Kiku took the controls.

Back on Earth, we ran to my house.

Chapter Two

The *Space Explorers* show was about a giant monster that could break up into four little monsters. Then it could go back to being one giant monster. The show was great.

At the end, Space Captain Zeke had big news.

"Hi, kids! We've made a *Space Explorers* video game. So buy a game and show people that you're one of us!"

I looked at Andrew. Andrew looked at Kiku. Kiku looked at Fuchsia. Fuchsia looked at me.

We were all thinking the same thing.

"I'm going home to ask my dad to buy one for me right now," said Fuchsia.

"Me, too!" I shouted.

My friends left, and I rushed into the kitchen. It was time for lunch. Dad looked up from his paper. He put his hand to his mouth, puffed up his cheeks, and burped.

"Sorry, Little Bill. I ate all the hot dogs. Maybe your mother will open a can of lima beans for you."

Dad knows how much I hate lima beans.

"Yuck," I said. "I would rather eat dirt."

"Dirt must taste better than it used to," he said.

My dad was always making jokes.

"Dad," I asked, "can I have a *Space Explorers* video game?"

"Sounds like fun. How much is it?"

"About fifty dollars," I said.

Dad looked surprised. "If I promise never to feed you lima beans, will you forget about the *Space Explorers* game?" He grinned.

"Please, Dad. I NEED this game."

My father scratched his head. "Go ask your mother," he said.

"Yes!" I said.

There was still a chance.

I went into the living room. Mom was putting pink flowers into water.

"Dad said that I should ask you if we can get a *Space Explorers* video game."

Mom smiled. "Do we need one?"

"It's really fun," I explained, "and it only costs fifty dollars."

Mom lost her smile. "That's a lot of money," she said. "Little Bill, I don't think we can buy it right now. Maybe for Christmas or your birthday."

"But Space Captain Zeke just told us about it. All the other kids are asking for one. Maybe the store will run out."

"Asking and getting are two different things, Little Bill. Fifty dollars is a lot of money for a toy."

I started feeling sad.

"Now, honey," Mom said. "I'm not saying no. I'm saying not right now. I'll talk to your father. Okay?"

"Okay," I said.

I had one last hope — my great-grandmother, Alice the Great. She was sitting in her rocking chair. Alice the Great always said yes to me.

"Great-Grandma," I said, "can you tell Dad to buy me a video game?"

"A video game?" she asked.

Uh-oh. She didn't sound happy.

"If you asked your father for a book, I would tell him it was a good idea. But a video game? I don't think so."

I couldn't believe it.

Without the video game, I'd never be a good Space Explorer. I felt like an alien in my own house. No one understood.

I went back into the kitchen.

"Hey, champ," Dad said. "Do you still want that dirt? How about a hot dog instead?"

I wasn't going to get the video game, but at least I could have a good lunch.

Chapter Three

After lunch I went back to the lot. Fuchsia and Kiku were already there. They looked unhappy, too.

"I told my dad that I would set the table every night if he bought the game for me," said Fuchsia. "He still said no."

"My dad said there are too many toys these days," said Kiku.

"So, what's wrong with toys?" I said.

We sat around and felt sad together. Just then, Andrew came running toward us.

"I got the game," he said. "Let's go to my house and play it!"

"Let's go!" we shouted.

At Andrew's house, we took turns playing the game. We must have caught a hundred aliens. The game was easy. Pretty soon we all had perfect scores.

Fuchsia always said what she was thinking: "I'm getting bored."

"Me, too," I said.

"Sorry, Andrew," said Kiku.

Andrew shrugged. "We can still play Space Explorers at the lot."

We ran to our spaceship and flew to the moon this time. We chased an alien that looked like a cat, but never caught it. Then we became the aliens. We jumped and ran and hid.

Soon the sun was going down. It was time to go home for dinner.We became Space Explorers again and left the moon. I was very tired when I finally reached my front door.

"Where have you been?" Mom asked.

"Saving the world from the aliens," I said.

"Thank you," Mom said. "I'm sure that the world is a much safer place. Now go wash the alien dirt off your hands."

"It's moon dirt," I said.

She laughed. "Okay, moon dirt. Dinner is almost ready."

Later that night, when Mom tucked me in, I told her about the video game. "We all took turns playing. It was fun. But you know what?"

"What?" she asked.

"It was more fun to play outside with my friends. I like to pretend. I don't need the game anymore," I said.

"I'm glad," Mom said. "Now go to sleep. Space Explorers need their rest."

She kissed me.

So I went to sleep and I dreamed of flying far into space with my friends. There were monsters shaped like lima beans and spaceships made of hot dogs.

HOWARD L. BINGHAM

HOWARD L. BINGHAM

Bill Cosby is one of America's best-loved storytellers, known for his work as a comedian, actor, and producer. His books for adults include *Fatherhood, Time Flies, Love and Marriage* and *Childhood.* Mr. Cosby holds a doctoral degree in education from the University of Massachusetts.

Varnette P. Honeywood, a graduate of Spelman College and the University of Southern California, is a Los Angeles-based impressive genre painter. Her work is included in many collections throughout the United States and Africa and has appeared on adult trade book jackets and in a children's book, *Let's Get the Rhythm of the Band.*

Books in the LITTLE BILL series:

The Meanest Thing to Say
All the kids are playing a new game.
You have to be mean to win it.
Can Little Bill be a winner...
and be nice, too?

The Treasure Hunt
Little Bill searches his room
for his best treasure.
What he finds is a great big surprise!

The Best Way to Play
Little Bill and his friends want the new *Space Explorers* video game.
But their parents won't buy it.
How can Little Bill and his friends have fun without it?